The Emma

When Emma falls downstairs and bumps her head, she suddenly finds another 'transparent' Emma at her side. Now there are two of her, will life be twice the fun? Certainly, the 'other' Emma is always up to tricks and the two of them are keen to confuse everyone in sight. But when the 'other' Emma starts causing havoc at school and Emma herself becomes the victim of her double's pranks, she really *is* in a dilemma.

Also by Catherine Sefton
in Magnet Books:

THE STRANGERS ON THE HILL
EMER'S GHOST
ISLAND OF THE STRANGERS

The Emma Dilemma

CATHERINE SEFTON

Illustrated by Jill Bennett

A Magnet Book

First published in Great Britain 1982
by Faber & Faber Limited
Magnet paperback edition published 1984
by Methuen Children's Books Limited
11 New Fetter Lane, London EC4P 4EE
Text © Catherine Sefton 1982
Illustrations © Faber & Faber Limited, 1982
Printed in Great Britain
by Cox & Wyman Ltd, Reading

ISBN 0 416 46800 4

A Book
to
make
CLARE SHERRARD
smile
when
she
is
big
enough
to
read
it!

Contents

If there were two of you,
  would you have twice the fun?

"I'm Emma," said Emma.
"But I'm Emma," said
Emma.
"You can't be," said
Emma.
"But I *am*," said
Emma.

And that was the Emma Dilemma.

Chapter One

Dracula's Revenge

Emma K. Small had a strange feeling in her bones from the moment she woke up. She knew there was something odd about the day. Something was going to happen.

"That's nonsense!" she told herself sharply. "It is an ordinary day, I am going to get out of bed in the ordinary way, and nothing is going to happen."

So she jumped out of bed . . . that was her ordinary way . . . and landed on the cat. Emma didn't know that her brother William's cat was snoozing on her Snoopy slippers before she landed on him, but she knew all about it afterwards.

"What did you jump on Dracula for?" William Small demanded indignantly, diving into Emma's room to rescue his cat, who was crouching behind the doll's house, licking bits of Emma off his claws.

"Oh! Oh! Oh!" Emma sobbed angrily, as she hopped around on one foot, trying to inspect her badly scratched knee. "Ow, Dracs! You rotten cat!"

"He is not a rotten cat," said William. "He is the

Prince of Darkness, and you deserved his Dreaded Scrab, so there!"

"You wait!" said Emma. "I'm going to get you, William!"

"You and what army?" said William, and he went off downstairs, clutching his cat and sucking his thumb. Downstairs, he complained to Mrs. Small about people who didn't look where they were jumping. Dracula Small was William's personal and private cat, and William didn't take kindly to people crash-landing on his property.

"Never mind, William," said Mrs. Small. "Have a Secret Toffee!" Mr. Small was a dentist and didn't like his children to eat sweets, but Mrs. Small sometimes stretched a point.

Emma came down to breakfast with her knee covered in iodine and sticking plaster and her mind set on revenge.

"Pax, Em!" said Mae Small, when she saw the glint in Emma's eye. Mae was the eldest of the Smalls' three children, and she acted as peacemaker and self-appointed Small Organizer in the holidays. "No bashing little brother!" she added firmly.

"I wouldn't dream of *bashing* William," said Emma cunningly, with all her fingers firmly crossed. She wasn't going to bash William, but she was going to get him.

"Of course Emma wouldn't!" said Mrs. Small, smiling hopefully.

"Wouldn't she?" said Mae.

"Mum," said Emma, "if you get your leg poisoned from a cat scratch, does it go black and fall off?"

"Of course not, dear!" said Mrs. Small.

"Don't change the subject, Em!" said Mae, who wasn't as easy-going as her mother.

"And don't call me 'Em'!" said Emma crossly.

There were three plates of porridge on the kitchen table. One for Emma, one for Mae, and one for William. Mrs. Small and Mr. Small had already eaten, because Mr. Small had to make an early start drilling holes in people's teeth.

Emma looked at the porridge, and smiled. She had had a Happy Thought.

She opened the door of the fridge.

Buttermilk.

She tasted it, and it tasted even nastier than she had expected. It was sour and horrible . . . exactly right for what she wanted.

She added the buttermilk carefully to William's porridge, and sat back to await results.

William was the smallest of the Smalls, and he always ate a lot in the hope of catching up on Emma. He took a very large spoonful of sour buttermilk and porridge.

"Uaarrggh! Ugh! Oooaugh!" he spluttered.

"Isn't your porridge nice, William?" asked Emma sweetly.

"William?" said Mae. "William, what's the matter?" She quickly fetched him a glass of water.

"Ough!" he said. "Oaaagh! Somebody's been mucking about with my porridge!"

"Have they?" said Emma innocently.

Mae tried the porridge.

"Yuk!" she said. Then: "*Emma?*"

"Me?" said Emma.

"Who else?" said Mae.

William said nothing, but he wasn't going to take it lying down. If Emma wanted a fight she could have one, no porridge barred.

"Peace in Smalldom, you two!" Mae warned, before they left the kitchen. "Your rotten little jokes aren't funny!"

"That means that *you* have to be nice to *me*, William," said Emma.

"Wait and see what happens," said William.

What happened, happened when she put on her Secrets Hat.

Emma's Secrets Hat had a hidden compartment, in the lining, where she kept things like stamps and bus tickets and lists. Emma liked making lists. She had made a list of PEOPLE I LIKE (her mother and Clare Sherry) and PEOPLE I DON'T LIKE (Busy Bee Bodley, and William, and Jammy Ogle, and Prue Rice) and PLACES I HAVE BEEN (The Natural History Museum in London and the Lake District and Belfast City Hall) and PLACES I WANT TO GO TO (Paris and Disneyland and An Island Where It Is Very Hot With Coconuts And No Spiders) and PLACES I DON'T WANT TO GO TO (School and School and School). She was sure that one day the lists would come in handy. If she married a millionaire and he asked her where she would like to go for her honeymoon she would take off her hat and look at her list, and then she would know. It would be Paris or Disneyland or An Island Where It Is Very Hot With Coconuts And No Spiders . . . it might even be all *three*, if he was a very rich millionaire. Emma's lists were Top Secret, so she never wrote them at home.

13

She wrote them in Clare Sherry's hut.

She wanted to add: "Put Buttermilk in Porridge" to her list of JOKES I HAVE PLAYED ON PEOPLE and so she was very anxious to put her hat on and go down the garden and climb over the wall into the Sherrys' garden, where the hut was.

Emma put her hat on.

Someone had filled it with porridge and buttermilk.

It ran down her neck, in dollops. It got into her ears and up her nose and all over her tee shirt.

"William!" Emma cried.

She darted out of her room and was in full Get-William flight when she came to the top of the stairs, where she failed to notice Dracula Small, who was having a siesta on the top step.

Yeeeellll!!!

C-R-U-N-C-H-!

Dracula went left, with a hiss and a screech and a vague notion that his world was coming to an end.

Emma plunged straight on down the stairs, *Crash-Bang-Wallop-SMACK*!, head-over-heels down thirteen steps to the landing, where she cracked her head against the wall, and promptly forgot all her problems.

Chapter Two

The Other One

Emma was lying on the landing. She opened her eyes.

Another Emma was sitting on the stairs.

"Hullo," said Emma on the stairs.

"Hullo," said Emma, dully. She had a very sore head and a buttermilk-and-porridge taste in her mouth. She felt as if she were half where she was, half somewhere else. "I'm in a dream!" she decided. "I *must* be in a dream, otherwise that Other One wouldn't be there."

The Other One was odd. She was transparent, and flickery round the edges. She came and she went. One minute Emma could see her clearly, and the next she couldn't.

"Who are you?" Emma asked the One-on-the-stairs.

"I'm Emma," said Emma.

"But I'm Emma," said Emma.

"You can't be," said Emma.

"But I *am*," said Emma.

"I AM," repeated the One-on-the-stairs, indignantly. "You're not!" And she flickered brightly making Emma blink.

15

"Yes I am!"

"No you're not!"

"If I'm not me, who am I then?"

"I *think*," said Emma-on-the-stairs, flickering doubtfully, "I *think* you are in one of my dreams. Anyway, *you* are not *me*!"

"I never said I was. I'm *me*. You're *you*. But who are you?"

"I'm Emma," said the Other Emma, with a defiant shimmer. Emma could see the stair carpet through the Other Emma, and the shimmering upset the pattern.

"No, I'm Emma," said Emma firmly.

"But I'm Emma," repeated the Other One.

And then wooziness and sleepiness flooded over Emma again and she went slipping back into unconsciousness, no longer caring where she was or what was happening to her.

Chapter Three

Two Emmas?

"Are you all right, Emma?" Mr. Small asked. He had dashed upstairs from the surgery to see his damaged daughter. Emma was lying on the sofa in the sitting-room, with a rug pulled up around her neck.

"Think so, Dad," she said.

"Shouldn't go parachute-jumping downstairs without a parachute," Mr. Small said, in the cheerful voice he used to calm down his victims. "You look as if you'll live!"

"She's got a big bump on her head," said William, admiring it.

"It hurts," said Emma slowly. She had a half-memory of *something* that had happened, and of talking to someone, but she couldn't think who.

"The Busy Bee says you never look where you're going at school," said Mae. "Now you're doing the same thing at home."

Emma frowned. The Busy Bee wasn't her favourite person.

"You're not at school now," said Mr. Small, relaxing

17

as he began to feel Emma was all right. "I think Miss Bodley will be welcoming you back next term."

"She doesn't like school, do you, Emma?" William said.

"Who does?" said Emma.

"No battered brains, or bones broken?" Mr. Small asked, looking at his watch. He had a waiting-room full of sore teeth to attend to, but he wasn't going back downstairs until he was sure Emma was in one piece.

"I feel all right, apart from my head," said Emma. She started testing bits and pieces to see if they were all in working order. The headache was the only problem. Her head felt as if she had been trying to knock down walls with it . . . which, of course, she had.

The surgery bell rang, summoning Mr. Small back. Mrs. Small had been left downstairs to hold the fort.

"Take it easy, Emma," Mr. Small advised, and he went off downstairs.

"Is Emma all right?" Mrs. Small said, bustling into the room.

"Yes," said Emma, putting a brave face on it.

"I'm not going to say anything about porridge, Emma, or teasing your brother, but I know the whole story."

"It was William's fault. I tripped over his old cat!"

"Don't try to blame other people, Emma. I've told you before about encouraging that cat to sleep in your bedroom."

"I like to hear him purr," Emma said. "He likes my slippers. He sleeps on them."

"Dracula is William's pet, not yours."

"Then William ought to look after him," said

Emma. "Dracula shouldn't have been on the stairs."

"And you two shouldn't have been having porridge fights!" said Mrs. Small. "Remember what Miss Bodley said in your report?"

Emma was unlikely to forget her report. It had been a very bad one.

"Nobody pays attention to the Busy Bee," Emma said.

"Don't they! I do. She's too soft with you. It's different at the Secondary School, Mae will tell you that!"

"Miss Bee Bodley's School is for babies!" said Mae.

"That's enough, Mae," said Mrs. Small, and she gave Emma a Secret Toffee. "Don't tell your Dad. He'll only say it will rot your teeth!"

The surgery bell rang again, and Mrs. Small buttoned up her Receptionist's coat and rushed downstairs to duty.

"When you grow up, don't marry a dentist!" she said to Mae as she left.

"I am grown up," said Mae.

"You're nearly thirteen," said William. "That's not grown up. That's hardly any grown-up-er than we are!"

"Oh, go away and suck your thumb somewhere," said Mae. William put his thumb in his mouth and went off to congratulate Dracula on a job well done.

Mae looked at Emma. Mae wanted to be a nurse when she left school, and Emma looked nurse-able.

"I wonder if I should take your temperature?" she said, in her best bedside manner.

"No thank you," said Emma, hurriedly.

"I'll get you a healthy orange drink," said Mae. "Lie there, and don't move!"

She went off to the kitchen.

One way to make sure that Emma *didn't* do something was to order her to do it. She stood up, shakily, and looked at herself in the cracked mirror over the mantelpiece. William had cracked it, firing marbles at his Action Man.

"Porridge!" she said, looking at her hair.

She limped off to the bathroom, and rinsed her hair. It was brown and curly, and porridge streaks didn't go well with it.

Then she decided to go up to her room to see what had happened to her Secrets Hat. She started to run up the stairs, but her head was still sore, and so she stopped and went more slowly. She reached the landing and opened the door of her room. But she didn't go in.

Instead, she stopped in the doorway, gazing across the room in amazement.

Her mouth dropped open.

"Oh!" Emma gasped.

That is, Emma standing-by-the-door gasped.

"Hi!" said Emma sitting-on-the-bed, cheerfully.

Chapter Four

Emma Em-Visible!

There were two of them.

Emma was sitting on the bed, and Emma was standing by the door. The Emma on the bed was transparent, and flickery round the edges, but she was undoubtedly *an* Emma, looking exactly the same as the first one.

Emma goggled at her.

"Where have you been?" asked Emma on the bed.

"Oh, gosh!" said Emma by the door.

There couldn't be *two* of her. It was impossible. But there was the Other Emma, sitting smiling on the bed, looking real, except that Emma could see the bed-post through her, and the curtains, and the wardrobe.

"I can . . . I can see through you!" Emma stuttered.

"Can you?" said Emma on the bed. She lifted up her hand and held it in front of her face, gravely inspecting it. "I *can't* see through me," she said.

Emma could see through the hand to the face, and right through the face to the yellow curtains on the window.

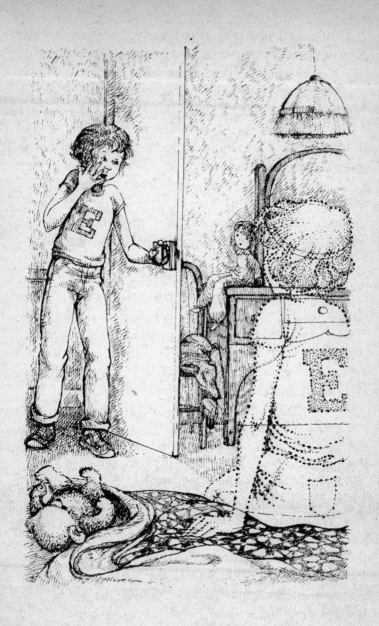

"I'm glad I can't see through me," said the Emma on the bed. "It would be a very yucky feeling, being able to see through yourself, wouldn't it?"

"Yes," said Emma, confirming by a quick glance that she was solid.

"Are you sure you can see through me?" asked Emma on the bed, sounding not very pleased. "I look quite normal to me."

"Yes, I can. I certainly can! I can see the curtains through you."

"Oh, can you? That makes me the EM-visible Emma! Well, now I'm going to make you something. Turn into . . . turn into an elephant."

"What?" said Emma blankly.

"Go on," said Emma on the bed. "Turn into an elephant. If *I'm* EM-visible *you* can be an elephant!"

"Why should I be?" asked Emma.

"If you're in my dream, you should do what I tell you," said Emma on the bed. "Go on, turn into an elephant."

Emma on the bed sat staring at Emma by the door, who felt embarrassed by it all. If she had been able to, she would have turned into an elephant out of politeness.

"Go on," said Emma on the bed. "This is my dream. I'm dreaming that you've come into my room looking exactly like me and saying that I'm transparent. Now you're going to turn into an elephant! Go on, turn."

"Your room?" said Emma.

"My room," said Emma on the bed.

"No," said Emma. "It's not! This is my room. And if there's any dream going on, it belongs to me!"

24

"I've decided I don't like this dream," said Emma on the bed. "I've never had a dream like this before. You're not behaving properly, for a person in a dream."

"If it is a dream," said Emma, feeling very confused.

"It must be a dream!" Emma on the bed said firmly. "I know, because I can see two of me! I mean, of us! You look *exactly* like me. There can't be two of me, so it *must* be a dream."

They stopped and looked at each other, thinking about it.

"Perhaps we're twins," said Emma on the bed, suddenly. "If we were twins, you could have been kidnapped at birth, and now you've come back to claim your rightful inheritance!"

Emma shook her head, and then winced, because it was still sore.

She knew that she was the *real* Emma. The Other Emma was transparent, and flickery round the edges. The trouble was that Emma on the bed didn't believe she was transparent, and Emma didn't like to mention it again. She knew that she wouldn't like it if someone went on and on about seeing the curtains through her.

"Listen," said Emma on the bed, and she recited: 'My name is Emma K. Small. I live at 37 Church Street, Balmayne. I attend St. Thomas's Primary School, Shore Street, Balmayne, and my teacher is Busy Bee Bodley whom I do not like."

"Snap!" said Emma by the door.

Emma on the bed looked cunning.

"All right," she said. "What does the 'K' stand for, then?"

25

" 'Kirstie'," said Emma. Her name was Emma Kirstie Small, but she called herself Emma K. Small because people like Jammy Ogle might make jokes about her if they knew she had a funny name. Emma didn't know anybody else called Kirstie. The Busy Bee said "Kirstie" was a very beautiful name, but Emma would rather have been called Ann or Mary or Karen Lesley like everybody else.

"I'm tired of this," said Emma on the bed. "Go away! Get out of my dream!"

Emma didn't say anything. She faced the Other, flickering Emma, trying to concentrate on her, and not the curtains, which could be seen through her and were most disconcerting.

"I *command* you to go away!" said the transparent Emma. "I'm going to close my eyes and count to ten, and when I open them you will have gone away!"

She closed her eyes.

"One! Two! Three! Four! (Emma by the door shuffled her feet, but the transparent Emma kept on counting) Five! Six! Seven! Eight! (Emma by the door coughed politely, and prepared to smile) Nine! TEN! There! You're GONE!"

She opened her eyes.

"You're not!" she said, sounding peeved. "You're a rotten awful nightmare, and I want it to end. I don't like nightmares."

Emma didn't like being called a nightmare.

"Emma!" Mae called up the stairs. "Em! I told you to stay on the sofa! Where have you disappeared to?"

"I've got to go now, that's my sister," said both the

26

Emmas, together. Then they stopped, and looked at each other.

"We'll find out who's real now!" said the transparent Emma triumphantly.

They both ran downstairs.

"Mum told you to stay still, Em!" Mae said accusingly. "Here's your orange drink!"

Mae walked straight past the outstretched hand of the transparent Emma and handed the glass of orange juice to Emma.

"Thank you," said Emma, with a mixture of relief and triumph in her voice.

The Other Emma stood stock still, staring at Mae and Emma. Her bottom lip began to quiver.

"She didn't see you!" said Emma, unable to restrain herself.

"What?" said Mae.

"Who were you talking to?" asked Mae.

"I wasn't talking to you," said Emma.

Emma was looking at the Other Emma, who had gone all shimmery, and cross. She looked as if she would either burst into tears or throw something.

"Is there anything the matter, Em?" Mae asked.

"It's all right," Emma said to the Other Emma. "Don't do anything silly."

"I'm not going to do anything silly!" said Mae. "You're the one who puts buttermilk in porridge and parachutes downstairs."

"Don't!" said Emma, sounding alarmed.

The Other Emma was advancing on her, shimmering dangerously.

"Don't worry, I won't," said Mae, who had no

intention of jumping downstairs, with or without a parachute. She thought that this was a peculiar conversation, but put it down to Emma's knock on the head. "Go and lie down on the sofa, Em," she said, in her best bedside manner, firm but gentle.

Emma backed away from Mae.

Suddenly, her arm jerked upwards, and the glass of orange juice flew out of her hand. It didn't fall to the ground. It rose, slowly, above Emma's head, and tilted.

Orange juice splashed down on top of her.

"Emma!" Mae exclaimed.

The glass slowly righted itself, and drifted down to the table. It landed with a faint rattle.

"You rotten stupid thing!" Emma shouted, dripping orange juice. "Look at me! I'm soaked! You're mean!

You're bad-tempered! You're . . . "

"No, I'm not," said Mae, bewildered.

First she had seen Emma's glass gently up-end itself over Emma's head, and now she was being blamed for it and called names.

"I'm going to get you!" Emma shouted at the Other Emma, ignoring her sister.

The Other Emma flickered out of the door, leaving Emma dripping orange juice, and Mae totally confused.

"I didn't do it, Em!" Mae said indignantly.

"I know you didn't do it!" fumed Emma.

"Then what are you shouting at me for?"

"I . . . oh!" Emma stopped, and thought about it. Mae couldn't see the Other Emma, so Mae didn't know what had happened.

"It was *an accident*, Mae," Emma said carefully. "The glass slipped out of my fingers. I dropped it, and it splashed me with orange juice."

"But it didn't!" said Mae. "If you drop something, it goes down. Your glass went up, and tilted, and poured over you. Then it came down!"

"You poor thing," said Emma, finding something to enjoy in the situation, even if she was dripping orange juice. "You're beginning to go batty! It happens with old age, you know, and you're almost thirteen!"

"Shut up, Em," said Mae, in a warning voice. At first, she had been certain that she had seen what she had seen. Now . . . she *couldn't* have seen it, could she? Doubt was beginning to creep in.

The only evidence was drippy Emma, who went on; "I expect the work is too hard for you in the

29

Secondary. Poor old thing! Mad! Who's going to tell Mum?"

Mae had had enough.

"I'm sick, Mae," Emma said, skipping round the side of the sofa as her sister advanced. "You're not allowed to do anything awful in case my head drops off!"

"All right," said Mae. "All right! I'll get you later."

Dracula Small didn't know what to make of it. He had been sitting in the hallway, carefully washing himself, when something Emma-like and flickering went past him.

"Hi, Dracs!" It said.

Dracula looked at it.

Dracula knew all the Smalls by sight and, more importantly, by smell.

This one had the right smell, but didn't look right at all. Was It his Emma, the Emma who owned his favourite Snoopy slippers, or was It not?

It went up the stairs.

Dracula paused in mid-paw-wash, startled. He could see the stairs through It. The experience was very upsetting, and enough to give a cat a nervous breakdown, if he had been a worrier. Dracula was not. He went back to washing himself.

Chapter Five

The Midnight Bells

Emma spent most of the day waiting for the Other Emma to strike again, but there wasn't so much as a shimmer.

"Sulking!" Emma decided, but she couldn't relax. She went to look for the Other Emma, because that was better than standing still and waiting to have glasses of orange juice poured over her.

"Emma?" she called, searching every corner in the house. "Emma?"

Mrs. Small began to get worried.

"Talking to herself!" she said to Mae, and she sent Emma to bed with an aspirin and a drink of water.

The remaining Smalls had their supper, and then Mr. Small put the lead on Dracula and walked the cat. After that he shut up the house and everybody went to bed, and to sleep.

Everybody except Emma. She couldn't get to sleep. She lay in the darkness counting sheep, and somehow, as she counted, the sheep all turned into Emmas, flickering, shimmering, transparent Emmas. Not

surprisingly, sleep wouldn't come.

Then . . .

. . . a bell rang.

It was the Surgery bell, which Mr. Small rang when he needed help. The bell had extensions to three or four parts of the house. They rang separately, one after the other.

Rrrrrrr!

Pause.

Rrrrrrr!

Pause.

Rrrrrrr!

Pause.

And then a final

RRRRRRRRRRRRRRR!!!!

to make sure that everyone wakened up.

Mr. Small was first out of bed, heading downstairs for his precious Surgery five steps at a time. He was closely pursued by Mae, Emma, William and Mrs. Small, clutching a burglar-swotting walking-stick, which was the nearest thing to hand.

There was no one in the Surgery. Mr. Small checked his equipment, and his drugs, and Mrs. Small checked the petty cash. No sign of any disturbance.

"Well, I don't know," said Mr. Small. "What do you think caused that?"

"Something wrong with the bell?" suggested Mae, yawning.

They all inspected the bell.

"It looks all right," said Mr. Small. He didn't know much about electricity, so he couldn't be sure.

"Quite inexplicable," said Mrs. Small. "But it will

do no good losing sleep over it. Children! Bed!" Then she looked at Mr. Small. "And you, Bertie!" she added.

They all trooped off upstairs.

Twenty minutes later, when everyone had begun to snuggle down and get over to sleep, the bells rang again.

Rrrrrrr

Pause.

Rrrrrrr

Pause.

Rrrrrrr

Pause.

And

RRRRRRRRRRRRRRR!!!!!

The last ring was long and insistent. It was still reverberating as Mr. Small bounded off the bottom step into the hall, but it stopped abruptly as he came through the surgery door.

This time he carried out a very thorough investigation, crawling upside down beneath the Receptionist's table to trace the bell wires.

Nothing.

Up to bed.

Half an hour later . . .

Rrrrrrr!

Pause.

Rrrrrrr!

Pause.

Rrrrrrrrrrr!

Pause.

And *then*

RRRRRRRRRRRRRRR!!!!!!!!!!!!
RRRRRRRRRRRRRRR!!!!!
RRRRRRRRR!!!!
RRR!!!
RRRRRRRRRRRRRRRR!!!
RRRRRR!!!

The whole Small family stumbled sleepily downstairs, with the exception of Mrs. Small, who stayed in bed clutching the walking-stick. Mae went yawning into the kitchen, and put on the kettle for a cup of tea.

The bell stopped ringing as soon as Mr. Small came through the surgery door. He called the bell some terrible names, and went hunting for his pliers.

"You stop it!" Emma said, in a warning voice.

"Stop what?" said William, who hadn't been doing anything, as far as he knew.

"It's no joke!" said Emma sternly.

William stared at his sister. She seemed to be having a conversation with the filing cabinet.

"Stop it now!" said Emma.

"Emma?" said William.

The glass case containing the false teeth plaster casts suddenly opened, all by itself. The sets of teeth were laid out in a row. One by one, as William watched, the teeth chattered at him.

Emma sprang forward, and wrestled with the lid of the case. Finally she got it closed.

"Golly!" said William.

"Ghosts!" said William. "I knew it was ghosts!"

"Shut up, William," said Emma, as her father came bustling back in with his pliers, to snip the bell wires.

"There!" he said. "No more ringing bells tonight!"

35

They marched into the kitchen, though William paused to inspect the plaster-cast teeth.

"They didn't bite me," he reported.

"What didn't bite you?" asked Mae.

"Dad's teeth," said William.

Mr. Small wasn't listening. He was still thinking about the bell. "Some sort of electrical fault!" he said.

"Poltergeists!" said William. "Not ghosts! Poltergeists!"

Emma said nothing.

Bells . . . and teeth . . . and orange juice . . . what next?

"Do you believe in poltergeists, Dad?" asked William.

"I believe in electrical faults," said Mr. Small.

"Emma was talking to the filing cabinet," William said, but nobody was listening. Mr. Small was busy explaining that he didn't like electricity, and Mae was washing her cup, and Emma didn't want to know.

"Time we got to bed!" said Mr. Small.

"Good night, Dad," said Emma. "Hope you sleep tight this time."

She went back to her room, clutching her comforting mug of tea . . . it was an Aries mug, and Aries was her Birth Sign . . . and trying not to think about the Other Emma.

But she was given no chance to forget.

Someone had been hard at work on the mirror in her room, writing with shaving foam.

The can of foam lay abandoned on the bed. It was a large green can which belonged to Mr. Small, and it was intended for lathering chins, not leaving messages, but

the message on the mirror was quite clear.

LIST OF PEOPLE I AM GOING
TO GET

No. 1   YOU

No. 2   YOU

and

No. 3   YOU

Signed:

The
REAL

Emma K. Small.

Chapter Six

The Great Emma Hunt

"Emma?" said Clare, peering over the wall at her friend. "Coming over to my side, Emma?"

"No," said Emma.

"What's wrong with you?" said Clare. "You're very pale, and you sound cross."

"I've got a headache," said Emma. "I fell downstairs."

"That was yesterday," said Clare. "Mae told me when I came looking for you to go out. I went swimming, but she said you couldn't come."

"That was because I hurt my head," said Emma. "And it's still sore."

She went off down the garden path to her own house, leaving Clare feeling snubbed.

"I wish people wouldn't bother me," Emma muttered under her breath. She had spent most of the morning trying to persuade William that he hadn't seen her talking to a filing cabinet. It was a boring conversation, and it made her head feel even sorer.

"It's all *her* fault!" Emma told herself, but she *didn't*

38

tell anyone else, because she knew no one would believe her.

It was time for the Great Emma Hunt to begin again, but this time she would have to be careful that no one saw her talking to filing cabinets, or heard her calling Emma's name . . . yesterday it had led to an early bed and a worried Mum; if she did it again they might send for the Big White Van.

"Emma?" she called, looking in the waiting-room.

No Emma. No *Other* Emma, that is.

"Emma?" She looked carefully behind the curtains, and under the sofa, in case the Other Emma was lurking there.

No Other Emma, shimmering, flickering, teeth-chattering or otherwise.

"Where are you?" Emma said, exasperated. "Emma, if you're hiding somewhere, and can hear me, will you please appear? We have to have a serious talk about things!"

There was no response.

"No wonder I can't find her, seeing she's almost invisible," thought Emma. "But I *must* find her, before she does something awful.

"If I can't find her, nobody can!

"She's *exactly* like me, after all. She'll hide where I would hide.

"Where would I hide?"

The answer came to her immediately.

She went out of the kitchen, and ran down the garden path to the wall by the compost heap. She clambered into the Sherrys' garden, making for Clare's hut.

"Emma?" Emma pushed open the door. "Emma, are you there?" She blinked in the sudden darkness. "I know you're in here somewhere, Emma."

"Go away," said a voice which sounded exactly like her own.

"Where are you?" Emma peered round the hut. She could make out the old tyres Clare used for armchairs, and the table, which was made of milk crates, and Clare's cupboard.

Something flickered at her. The Other Emma was standing in the corner, by the window.

"What's the matter?" the Other Emma asked. "Can't you see me either?"

"Yes, I can, but not very clearly. You're still transparent, you see!"

"No, I don't see," said the Other Emma irritably. "I look quite ordinary to me."

"But not to anyone else," said Emma.

"Dracula can see me," said the Other Emma. "At least he *thinks* he can! His hair went prickly, and he stalked round me, and then he tried batting me, the way he used to bat a little paper ball when he was a kitten."

"Poor Dracs!" said Emma. "I don't think he's been up to sleep on my slippers since."

They both knew since *what*.

"It isn't fair!" the Other Emma said suddenly. "I don't see why you couldn't be the transparent one."

"It's not my fault," said Emma uneasily.

"Did you see my list? I'm going to get you!"

"What for?" asked Emma. "Just for being me?

40

Because I'm real and you're transparent, is that it?"

"I'm real too," said the Other Emma, "even if I am transparent."

Emma thought about it.

"You're real all right," she admitted reluctantly.

"Great!" said the Other Emma. "I believe in me. You believe in me. Dracs isn't quite certain. And the rest of the world doesn't want to know!"

"William thinks you're a poltergeist, and Dad thinks you're an electrical fault," said Emma. "He didn't know what to make of it when you kept on ringing that bell!"

The Other Emma giggled. "It was funny, wasn't it?"

Emma didn't want to offend the Other Emma, because then all sorts of things might happen, and *she* would be blamed for them. Emma didn't want to offend the Other Emma, but she didn't want to encourage her either.

"Y-e-s, it was funny," she said, not quite truthfully. "But it kept us up out of our beds, and Mum has been in a state all morning because she didn't get her sleep."

"Oh," said the Other Emma. "Sorry! I thought it was funny."

"Well, it was!" said Emma. "I mean, everybody dashing up and down like that, when all the time it was transparent old you pressing the button. And William's face, when you chattered the false teeth . . . lucky Mae and Dad didn't believe him."

"Dad couldn't see me," said the Other Emma. "I stood right next to him."

"*Dad*," thought Emma. *My* Dad . . . her Dad too. It was confusing, and she didn't like it very much. She

41

didn't want to share her family with the Other Emma, but now was the wrong time to argue about it. What she wanted to do was to get the Other Emma on to her side.

"Your joke with the bells was funny," she said carefully. "But you played it on the wrong people. Dad, and Mum, losing their sleep. It would be much better if we could play some of your jokes on people who deserve them."

"William deserves to be paid back for putting porridge in my hat," said the Other Emma thoughtfully.

My hat! Emma thought. Obviously both the Emmas had the same memories up to the time when Emma fell downstairs and banged her head, which meant they had the same enemies.

"We'll play some jokes on William," said the Other Emma.

"Yes. YES!" said Emma, brightening up. She had lots of ideas about things that could be done to William by a visible and an invisible Emma working together. "William and then Mae! We'll make it their Disaster Day!"

Chapter Seven

William-And-Mae Day

William had had a good morning. First he had been a Black Hand Commando and terrorized most of the people he knew in Balmayne, and then he had been down to Scrubb's Amusements, where he almost won the gold watch.

He came into dinner feeling cheerful.

"William, hands!" said Mae, in her bossiest big-sister voice.

William had to go upstairs and wash his hands. His right hand was not too bad but his left, the Black Hand Sign one, took a lot of scrubbing. When he came downstairs again, everyone else had started eating.

"I almost won the watch today," said William conversationally.

"Which means William has been down to Scrubb's again, and lost all his pocket money," said Mae unsympathetically.

"It's a very good watch," said William. "I bet I win it one day. I bet I . . . "

"Don't talk! Eat!" said Mae.

"Don't be so bossy, Mae," said Mrs. Small.

William looked at his dinner. Then he looked at Emma's dinner, or what was left of it, for Emma's dinner was rapidly disappearing. Then he looked at Mae's dinner, and his father's dinner, and his mother's dinner.

"Where are my sausages?" he demanded indignantly.

"What's that, William?" asked Mrs. Small.

"You've all got three sausages each. I haven't got any!" William looked very cross.

"Yes, you have," said Emma happily.

"No I haven't!" said William.

Then he saw his sausages.

They were sitting on top of his peas, where Mae had put them to begin with.

"Don't play silly games, William," said Mr. Small severely.

William said nothing. What could he say?

"Any seconds, Mum?" asked Emma, who had already cleared her plate. She helped herself to more peas and potatoes.

William chewed one of his sausages, and thought. Then he reached out for another one.

"Hey!" he said, his fork hovering over a sausage-less plate.

"What now, William?" said Mrs. Small.

"My sausages have gone again!"

"WILLIAM!" said Mr. Small, suddenly sounding very angry. "I will not have meals interrupted by your games!"

"That isn't one bit funny, William!" said Mrs. Small.

Then William saw what they were talking about.
His sausages were standing in his glass of water.

"Euhh!" said Mae. "You disgusting child, William!"

"Eat the rest of your dinner in the kitchen,
William," said Mr. Small.

William, and his wet sausages, retreated to the
kitchen. William was bewildered. He had been sitting
with bossy Mae on one side of him, and his father on
the other. Neither of them seemed likely sausage-
dippers.

He sat in the kitchen and ate his sausages (which
were none the worse for the dipping, only a bit greasy)
and tried to work out what had happened to him, but
he couldn't.

"William!" said Mae. "Did you fill my gardening
boots with wet sand?"

45

"No," said William.

"I think you did," said Mae. "Somebody did!"

"Emma," said William.

"Emma hasn't been out of my sight since I took them off coming in from the garden. You have!" said Mae.

"I never touched your rotten boots," said William.

He said more or less the same thing about Mae's anorak when she found it hanging on the washing line, stuffed with grass cuttings, with the arms tightly knotted together.

"Just ONE more of your tricks, William, and REAL trouble!" fumed Mae.

"I can't reach the line!" wailed William.

"Oh, disappear, or something!" said Mae.

William did as he was told. He was afraid of Mae when she was cross.

He went upstairs to the sitting-room to sulk. He was nowhere near the vase of flowers when it rose off the window-ledge and tipped itself over Dracula, drenching the Prince of Darkness with a cascade of roses and water.

"WILLIAM!" said Mrs. Small, surveying the scene, and the soaking cat.

"It . . . it lifted!" William said.

"WILLIAM!" Mrs. Small seemed to swell.

"Has William made a mess of the carpet, Mum?" asked Emma, putting her head round the door.

"You keep out of this, Emma," said Mrs. Small. She sent William for the mop bucket.

He was carrying the mop and bucket through the kitchen from the yard when, somehow, the mop took on a life of its own. It wriggled in his hands, got between his legs, and tripped him up.

William fell over, landing in Dracula's milk dish, which broke.

Mop water, and milk, and bits of broken dish and Wailing William flooded everywhere.

"WILLIAM!" Mrs. Small arrived on the scene in a fine temper. "WILLIAM! WILLIAM SMALL! HOW COULD YOU!"

"D-d-d-d-on't know," wailed William, who truly didn't know how he could. He only knew that he had.

"Naughty William," said Emma primly, keeping well out of range of the mop which her mother was waving like a bayonet. She escaped from the fray, and wandered up the garden. Mae was working in the strawberry bed.

"Hullo," Emma said.

"Buzz off!" said Mae.

"Mind you don't trip, Mae," said Emma innocently.

And the next moment, Mae did trip . . . or she was shoved, she could never be quite certain which. She was walking up the path past the compost heap at the time, and there was no one near her, so she must have tripped.

She stumbled, and sat down.

In the compost heap.

"I warned you," said Emma. "I *somehow* knew you were going to trip just then, Mae. Aren't I clever?"

Rotten cabbage and garden rubbish and tea leaves and all sorts of unspeakable things had gone into the compost heap, and most of them came out again, attached to Mae.

"Oooh!" Mae stood there, cloaked in compost.

47

"You do look a mess, Mae," said Emma happily.

Then she darted down the path to the house before the Thing From the Smalls' Compost Heap could catch her.

The Thing retreated to the bathroom, squelching down the garden path and leaving a give-away trail of compost footprints on the path. On the path, they were all right. It was when Mrs. Small followed them up the stairs to the bathroom that the trouble began.

"My children have all gone mad!" Mrs. Small muttered, throwing carbolic over Mae with one hand and holding her nose with the other.

Mae was not a pretty smell.

"Wasn't that brilliant?" said the Other Emma when she met Emma, as arranged, on the promenade. "Mae will be smelly for days!"

"My best ever joke on Mae," said Emma.

"*My* best ever joke," corrected the Other Emma. "You watched from a safe distance, where she couldn't get her mucky hands on you!"

"I was establishing an alibi," said Emma. "Who thought of it, anyway?"

"*Our* best ever joke," said the Other Emma. "What are we going to do next?"

Prue Rice, who was fat, was having a little private picnic on the beach. Little Private Picnics were how she had become fat in the first place.

Someone put green seaweed in her lettuce sandwiches.

Prue didn't like it.

Then, somehow, she sat on her banana.

It came up very squashed, because there was a lot of Prue.

She went home for another banana . . . or two.

Shortly after that, things started to go wrong for Jammy Ogle.

Jammy had appointed himself Castle Knocker Down for the day. He went up and down the beach finding little kids and kicking down their castles. It was a good game, for Jammy, because he was very big and the kids were very little.

"Building castles, Fish Face?" Jammy said to Emma, and he kicked Emma's castle.

There was a stone inside it.

"Ohohoho! I've broke my foot!" Jammy cried, hopping round on one leg.

He wasn't sure where the jellyfish came from, but three of them arrived, one after the other.

49

Splat!

Splat!

Splat!

Jammy retreated, shedding jellyfish, to inspect his sore toes.

Someone let down Hector Smith's bicycle tyres, and filled his saddlebag with Kentucky Fried Chicken papers.

Someone poured sea water into Lindy Scullion's lemonade.

Then . . .

"William!" breathed the Other Emma delightedly.

William appeared on the promenade, grinning happily.

Life had begun to look up for him after the morning's disasters. First of all Mrs. Small gave him a Secret Toffee, after she had mopped up the cat's milk. "Don't tell your father!" she warned him. Then Mr. Small, who had heard the distant roars of battle, intercepted him in the hall and gave him 20p. "To cheer yourself up with. But don't tell your Mum, eh?"

"Great, Dad!" said William.

He arrived on the promenade clutching a Chocolate Whirry Big Size with 2p of dip on top. It was the biggest ice cream he had ever seen.

William opened his mouth, and raised the ice cream to it. Then, at the vital moment, the ice cream *wriggled*, and plunged forward, out of his hand.

"Oh, William! What *are* you doing with an ice cream cornet stuck on your nose?" asked Emma sweetly.

Tears came to William's eyes.

He pulled the ice cream cornet off his nose, and

blinked unhappily at his Chocolate Whirry Big Size, or what was left of it. Most of it was on his nose, or dripping down on to his jersey.

"Didums dip ums nose?" teased Emma cruelly, and William threw the squashed cornet at her, and missed. He gave a big sniff and turned away, still dripping ice cream.

Emma felt a pang of conscience.

"William," she said, going after him. "William. I'm sorry about your ice cream, William. Stop crying, William. Let me wipe you up a bit with my hankie."

"I-I-I d-d-don't want your h-h-help," William sobbed, wiping his face with his sleeve, and sniffing hard. "You'd only play some rotten trick on me."

"I won't! Honestly, I won't!" said Emma, feeling guilty.

"Somebody is playing rotten tricks on me," said William. "I-I-I d-don't know how, but somebody is!"

"It won't happen again, William," said Emma. "I'm *sure* it won't," she added firmly.

William was still crying.

"The m-m-mop tripped me and I fell in D-Dracula's d-d-dish and smashed it and somebody hid my s-sausages and stirred my water with them and then my ice c-c-cream ju-ju-jumped on to my n-n-nose!"

"I think you are too small to have all those jokes played on you," said Emma. "Come on. I'll take you home to Mum."

She took her small brother by the hand and led him down the promenade.

"Don't hold my h-hand," William said. "I'll walk in front of you." He couldn't afford to have any of his friends in the Black Hand Commando see him hand in hand with his soppy sister Emma. He had his tear-stained and ice-cream-smeared dignity to consider.

"We shouldn't have done it!" Emma said to the Other Emma, who was walking along beside her, trying not to step on the cracks in the paving stones.

"It was your idea to get William," said the Other Emma.

"It wasn't!" said Emma hotly.

"Liar!" said the Other Emma.

"Who are you calling a liar?" said Emma, stopping.

"You said we'd have William-and-Mae Day!" said the Other Emma. "So we threw Mae in the compost and we got William!"

"Y-e-s," admitted Emma. "But you thought of playing tricks first!"

52

A lady in a blue hat touched Emma gently on the arm. "Are you feeling all right, dear? You seemed to be talking to someone, throwing your arms about, and I was worried."

"She's my sister," said William, coming back to see what was the matter.

"Is your sister *all right*, dear?" asked the lady, in a whisper which Emma wasn't meant to hear.

William considered it.

"*Usually* she is," he said, beginning to cheer up again.

Emma spluttered.

"Ouch!" said William, as someone pinched him, hard! He thought it was a person, but it must have been a wasp . . . except that he couldn't see the wasp.

"Were you talking to someone, dear?" the lady asked.

"I was talking . . . " Emma began, and then the blue hat rose an inch or two off the lady's head, and dropped back on again, crookedly. "I was talking to myself!" Emma said, trying not to giggle.

"Talking to yourself, dear?" the lady asked, reaching up to steady her hat.

"Yes," said Emma. "Rehearsing. For a play."

"Oh," said the lady.

"I didn't know you were in a play," said William.

"Well, I am," said Emma.

"What play is it, dear?"

Emma didn't know much about plays.

"I don't know yet," she said. "I'm just rehearsing in case there is one, and in case I'm in it."

"I see," said the bewildered lady, and she went on her way thinking How Peculiar Children Are These Days. The Peculiar Child was relieved to see her go.

Emma and William and the Other Emma walked on down the promenade, with William a face-saving distance in front.

They were watched by the gleaming green eyes of Dracula Small, who was sunning himself beneath a veronica bush. He saw his friend William, and he saw Emma, and he saw It.

It was the one who smelled right but looked wrong.

It was the one who had tipped roses and water over him.

Dracula's fur bristled. He got up, stretched himself, and crept deeper into the veronica bush, just to be on the safe side.

"We've got to be nice to someone for a change," Emma was explaining to the Other Emma. "We've got

54

to make it up to William for all the tricks we've played on him."

"How?" asked the Other Emma.

Chapter Eight

Friends Or . . . ?

"Look at my watch!" said William, proudly displaying it. "I won it!" he added, trying to sound as if winning watches was an everyday William activity.

The family inspected the watch.

"You won at Scrubb's place?" said Mr. Small. "I didn't think anyone could win the big prizes down there."

Neither had the Hoop-la man.

William's ring had hovered over the watch, and then settled gently, with a final wriggle of adjustment. The Hoop-la man was very surprised.

"Never seen nothing like it!" he told Benjy Scrubb. "It went slow . . . like someone was carrying it, almost."

"See that it don't happen again!" said Benjy, scratching his bald head. "Them watches is for show, not for losing. If kids begin to win them, what next?"

"It's gold," William said. "Real gold! Isn't it, Dad?"

"It looks a very good watch, William," Mr. Small admitted.

"I told Emma I'd win it," said William. "That's why she gave me the money to try!"

"Emma gave you money to play Hoop-la?" Mae said. Emma and William spent most of their days fighting, not helping each other.

"I'm very pleased to hear it, Emma," said Mrs. Small, who was first to recover from the shock.

Mr. Small looked doubtful. He thought William had used the 20p he wasn't supposed to tell his mother about.

"Very kind of you, Emma," said Mrs. Small.

"Quite *amazing*," said Mae, in a voice which indicated that she didn't believe the story for a minute.

"I practised very hard to win it, of course," said William. "I'm very good at Hoop-la. I've developed a method. If any of you would like to win something, I'll be quite happy to help you."

Emma looked alarmed. "It mightn't work *twice*, William," she said nervously.

"They have great things on the Hoop-la," said William. "Diamond bracelets, and vases, and watches, of course. Well, they *had* a watch. But now they haven't, because I WON it! I'm going to go to the Hoop-la every Saturday with my pocket money and win Christmas presents for you all."

"Thank you, dear," said Mrs. Small.

Emma escaped to the garden, leaving William displaying his gold watch to Miss Bee Bodley, who had dropped in with her Dr. Barnardo's collecting box.

Clare was in the garden next door.

"Hullo," Emma said.

"Hi," said Clare.

"Can I come over?"

Clare looked surprised. "I thought you were too busy to come over, these days."

"No," said Emma, and then she realized that she hadn't seen Clare properly since the Other Emma began to take up so much of her time. "That is, I have *been* rather busy, but now I'm not."

"Oh," said Clare. "Aren't you?"

"Can I come over? We could do something in the hut."

"Could *we?*" said Clare, tossing her head. "I'm afraid I can't play with you today, Emma. I've far too much to do."

Clare went back into her own house.

"Now see what you've done!" Emma said to the Other Emma, who was sitting on the swing.

"Not my fault!" said the Other Emma, shimmering. "Clare can't even see me!"

"I don't want to play any more tricks," said Emma. "It was funny to start with, but now it isn't. I think no more tricks."

"Oh, do you?"

"Yes, I do!"

"You can't give me orders!" said the Other Emma. "You're getting as bad as Bossy Mae. I do what I like. You think that just because people can see you and they can't see me you're one up."

"I never said I was," said Emma.

"But you meant it, all the same," said the Other Emma. "You think you can boss me. Well, you can't. I'll do what I want to do, when I want to do it. Not what you tell me." She flickered fiercely round the edges.

"I wasn't trying to be bossy . . . "

"You'd better watch out!" the Other Emma interrupted her. "Remember you're still on my list."

The Other Emma got off the swing and went down the path, slamming the garden gate behind her. For a sort-of ghost, which is what Emma had decided she was, the Other Emma had a very strong gate-slam at her command.

The gate-slam awakened Dracula, who had been snoozing beneath the rhubarb. He stretched himself, and looked at the Emma who was standing by the swing. Was it his Emma, the Emma of the comfy-to-sleep-on-Snoopy-slippers, or it?

She was his Emma. He knew she was, because he couldn't see through her. He purred, expectantly.

Emma paid no attention.

She was too busy thinking to notice Dracula. There had been enough jokes, but the Other Emma was too concerned with proving that a solid Emma couldn't be allowed to boss a transparent one to listen.

"I'll have to stop her somehow," Emma thought.

Chapter Nine

The Doing-It-Backwards Burglar

"Oh no!" said Emma, in dismay. She was in her room, staring at her bed.

The Other Emma had wasted no time thinking about what to do next. She'd done it.

It was a cruel joke, much worse than Emma had expected.

"No! No! No!" she muttered, clenching her fists.

Seaweed.

A mound of seaweed lay in the middle of her sheet. There was a note on top.

GOT YOU THIS TIME
BOSSY BOOTS!

It was in Emma's handwriting.

"But I didn't write it!" Emma thought. What could she do?

The immediate problem was how to dispose of the seaweed. The dustbin was the obvious place, but the Smalls' dustbin was always filled to overflowing.

"I could put it in Dad's wheelbarrow, and wheel it

down to the beach," Emma thought, not very happily. But thinking of the wheelbarrow made her think of the garden, and that made her think of Mae falling in the compost heap, and that was the solution!

The seaweed could go on the compost heap.

"Which is probably where she got it in the first place," Emma thought bitterly.

But how to get it there? She couldn't run the risk of lugging a sheet full of seaweed down the stairs and out to the end of the garden in daylight. Someone would be bound to see her, unless they all went out.

"I'll have to wait until they've all gone to bed!" Emma decided.

They had supper, and Mr. Small walked Dracula and fixed the burglar alarm, and then everybody went up to bed.

Emma got into bed with her clothes on under her nightdress, and waited. It was long past midnight when she decided it was time to move.

She slipped out of bed, and put on her dressing-gown and Snoopy slippers. Then she went downstairs, looking rather fat because of having her clothes on beneath her nightdress, and switched off the alarm. They had to have an alarm, back and front, because of the medicines in the Surgery, and Mr. Small's precious equipment.

Emma came back upstairs, wrapped the sheet round the seaweed, and carried the bundle carefully down-stairs, taking care not to leave a seaweed trail behind her.

She put the bundle down in the kitchen and checked

the window to see if there was any light from the house
shining across the yard or the garden. There wasn't, so
she slid back the bolt, opened the door, went down the
yard, and opened the gate into the garden.

C-r-e-a-k! Mr. Small had forgotten to oil it. Emma
froze, expecting lights to flash on, but nothing
happened.

She went back to the kitchen, and took up the seaweed bundle. It was heavy, but she had to carry it,
because she was afraid of the noise dragging it might
make, and the damage it would do to the sheet.

"Like a robber carrying his booty," she thought
with a shiver.

Through the garden gate, up the path just past the
two apples and the quince tree, level with the strawberry bed . . . and at last she was able to drop the

seaweed on to the compost heap, beside the Mae-shaped hole where her sister had landed.

"What a smell!" Emma thought, as she shook out the sheet. But what was she going to do with it? If she took it back into the house, it was likely to be found.

She folded it up tightly, and nipped over the wall into the Sherrys' garden. The hut had no lock, and she was able to hide the sheet away behind one of Clare's tyre armchairs, where no one but Clare would be likely to see it.

"Clare's my friend. She'll guess it was me. She won't give me away!"

Clare had *been* her friend. Now Emma wasn't so sure, which was yet another thing the Other Emma had to answer for.

Emma climbed back over the wall, and dropped into her own garden.

Mission accomplished! She felt like a secret agent making her way back to base through enemy territory. The quince tree was enemy headquarters, and the two apple trees were outposts. She evaded them both, and got through the garden gate without so much as a creak, although she didn't dare to close it fully.

The kitchen door was open, but the light was on.

"*Mum!*" Emma thought, and her heart sank down into her Snoopy slippers. Then she saw a flickering in the kitchen.

"Emma!" she breathed.

The Other Emma came to the doorway, shimmering and flickering as if she were enjoying herself.

"You rotten thing! You put that old seaweed on my bed and ruined it. My sheet was all stinky."

64

"Yah!" said the Other Emma, sticking her tongue out. "Serve you right for being bossy."

"I'll . . . I'll . . . " Emma stuttered, pink with rage.

Then she realized why the Other Emma was looking so pleased with herself.

"Emma!" she hissed urgently. "Don't!"

The Other Emma did.

She closed the kitchen door and fastened it on the inside, locking Emma out in the yard. Then the Other Emma made some very rude faces at her double through the kitchen window, before retreating further into the house, switching off the light behind her.

Emma was left in the darkened yard, speechless with rage. She was wearing her nightdress and dressing-gown, over her daytime clothes, and her Snoopy slippers. She had no torch, and it felt as if it were going to rain.

It was half past one in the morning and the rain had begun to fall heavily when Mr. Small was awakened by the burglar alarm, which the Other Emma had thoughtfully switched back on after she locked the back door.

Mr. Small galloped downstairs, complete with the burglar-bashing walking-stick, to find his daughter Emma stuck upside down in the window of the back pantry, breaking into her own house, like a doing-it-backwards burglar.

"What on earth were you doing, Emma?" he demanded, when he had removed the small wet girl from the window where she had stuck fast, partly because of all the clothes she was wearing.

"I . . . " Emma started, and then stopped. She was pretty good at excuses, but this one defeated her. Then, a brainwave.

"Sleepwalking!" she said.

"*Sleepwalking?*"

"I must have been sleepwalking," Emma said, congratulating herself. "I expect I went for a sleepwalk in the garden."

Mr. Small thought about it.

"What about the alarm?" he said. "How did you get out without it sounding?"

Emma frowned, then her brow cleared.

"Don't know," she said innocently. "I was asleep, wasn't I?" .

Her father looked at her hard.

"Were you?" he said.

"I wouldn't lock myself out, would I?" she said.

"Wait a minute!" said Mr. Small. "You were *locked* out! Somebody must have locked you out! You couldn't lock yourself out, could you? It isn't physically possible."

"I suppose not," said Emma, unhappily.

"What a stupid trick!" Mr. Small said. "Must have been William."

But William was sound asleep upstairs, and so was Mae.

They went back to bed.

"Emma can't have locked herself out," Mr. Small said, sitting up in bed with a mug of chocolate. "But she *was* outside, and soaked to the skin, with the door locked behind her."

66

Mrs. Small blinked at him sleepily.

"Something's going on here!" he muttered. "Bells ringing, children behaving peculiarly, and now this! I don't understand it!"

"Couldn't we go to sleep?" said Mrs. Small.

"Not till I've worked it out!" Mr. Small said.

But he couldn't solve the problem, and he had to go to sleep in the end.

Chapter Ten

Where Will I Strike Next?

Emma woke up late the next morning, with a sniffle to add to her sore head.

Someone had pulled out all the drawers in her chest of drawers, and emptied the contents in the middle of the floor.

Someone had knotted her tights together, toe to toe, and made a garland of them which stretched right across the room like a Christmas decoration.

Someone had upturned her Busy Lizzie plant in the middle of the piled-up clothes from the chest of drawers, and *someone* had written:

WHERE
  WILL
    I
      STRIKE
        NEXT?
       HA HA

in felt tip across the top of Emma's mirror.

Obviously, it was *someone's* idea of a joke!

Emma could have wept.

"This isn't fair!" she said, storming out of bed.

She stormed straight into the basin full of cold water and soap bubbles that *someone* had thoughtfully left for the purpose, just where Emma would step in it.

The soapy water swirled across the carpet and soaked into the clothes and the mud from the flower pot.

"Oh! Oh! Oh! Oh!" Emma stood, damp of foot and scarlet in the face, with tears brimming in her eyes. "It isn't funny. I hate you! I hate you! You and your mean rotten jokes! You're a horrible awful rotten nasty insect!"

A lot of footstamping and bad temper later, Emma had to start tidying the room. The alternative was to try to convince her mother that she'd done a second, destructive, sleepwalk, and she didn't want to try that because her father had already made enough fuss about the first one.

She re-potted the Busy Lizzie, and got as much of the mud as she could off her clothes before putting them back in the chest of drawers, somewhat damp and higgledy-piggledy, but out of sight, at least. Then she went to clean the mirror.

WHERE
  WILL
    I
      STRIKE
        NEXT?
        HA HA

The message was quite clear.

Emma . . . the Other Emma . . . was going to keep on playing tricks, and that meant that sooner or later there would be trouble.

Emma cleaned the message off the mirror, and sat down on the bed.

"She's exactly like me!"

Brainwave!

Emma had always known that her Secrets Hat lists would come in useful. Now, just when she needed them, she was able to unzip the secret compartment in her hat and turn up the 'List of People I Don't Like'.

LIST OF PEOPLE I DON'T LIKE

by Emma K. Small Ph.D., B.D., V.C., F.R.C.S.

REASONS WHY I DON'T LIKE THEM

W. Small	Because he is utterly rotten.
M. Small	Because she is bossy Small.
Winifred Epsley	Because she steals things.
Jammy Ogle	Because he is a bully.
Busy Bee Bodley	Because she doesn't like me.
Prudence Rice	Because she is too fat.

And All other People Who Are Unkind To Animals

© E.K. Small 1982

This List First Published E.K. Small 1982.
Not to be read by anyone else without special

permission from E.K. Small.

Unauthorised Readers will be PROSECUTED.

Signed
E.K. Small.
Ph.D., B.D., V.C.,
F.R.C.S.
(Author)

Emma studied the list.

Winifred Epsley could be crossed out because she was in Liverpool on her holidays, where she boasted that she would be able to steal better things from bigger shops.

Prue Rice had had her seaweed sandwiches, and William had had his ice-cream nose dip, and Jammy Ogle had run into a well-placed jellyfish or three, Splat! Splat! Splat! in the face. Bossy Small was still walking around smelling of carbolic and compost heap, despite all her mother's efforts and a large dose of the perfume her father had given her for her birthday.

That left Busy Bee Bodley, Headmistress of St. Thomas's Primary School, Shore Street, Balmayne.

Chapter Eleven

The Wrecking Of Classroom Nine

Beatrice Bodley, B.A., was small and fat and red-haired, and built like a pocket battleship. She wore purple stockings with silver butterflies on them and she was a very busy person. Everybody called her "Busy Bee".

She rode a red bicycle with panniers back and front. In the front one she kept her messages and in the back she had her artist's easel and painting things, just in case she saw something she wanted to paint. She stuck posters in her front window for Dr. Barnardo's and the R.S.P.C.A. and Keep Britain Tidy. She ran Jumble Sales for the Girl Guide Troop and she was Co-Founder of Balmayne Natural History Club and Chief Barker of the Moyadd and Balmayne Dog and Puppy Club. She was Secretary of the Association of Business and Professional Women and Sole Organizer of the Balmayne Fun Joggers and Fitness Through Health League; all of which didn't give her much time for growing mushrooms, except in the holidays. She grew mushrooms in the darkness of the boiler-house at St.

Thomas's Primary School. She kept them in trays where the coal used to be before the school went over to oil-fired central heating.

That morning Miss Bodley was in the boiler-house, wearing her white mushroom-growing gloves and trying to count her mushrooms, when she heard a disturbance in the empty school buildings.

"Vandals!" Miss Bodley thought.

She put down her mushroom tray and took off her gloves. Then she marched into the school and down the corridor to her own room, Classroom Nine, where the noise was coming from. She opened the door of the classroom and marched in, prepared to expel invaders.

The first thing she saw was the writing on the blackboard.

Miss Bodley's face went pale.

"Who did that?" she snapped. "Come out, wherever you are!"

She opened the door of the store-room. No one inside. She looked behind the blackboard. Then she looked at the board again.

I HATE B. BODLEY!

"Some silly infant!" she muttered. She lifted the blackboard duster to clean the writing off and then . . .

The door slammed shut, with a loud bang!

Miss Bodley walked over to it, and looked out, down the corridor.

"Wind?" she thought.

The light in Classroom Nine went on.

Miss Bodley blinked. The switch was just beside the door. She reached for it, but before her hand got there the switch flicked down, and off went the light.

And on again.

And off!

And on!

And off!

Then it stopped.

Miss Bodley was frozen to the spot. She had seen the light switch flick up and down. But . . .

A desk lid banged at the far end of the classroom.

Miss Bodley spun round.

Bang! Bang! Bang! Bang! One lid after another, up one row and down the next.

Then one of the cacti from the window ledge took off in a flight across the room, at Emma-height. It swooped towards Miss Bodley, who grabbed at it and missed.

"Stop it!" Miss Bodley shouted, badly shaken.

She went after the cactus, which zoomed towards her desk. She grabbed at it, and this time she caught it, just before it upturned over her desk. The plant resisted her, the pot twisting in her hands as though someone were trying to pull it out of her grasp.

"Stop it!" Miss Bodley demanded.

Whatever was holding the plant suddenly let go, and Miss Bodley tottered backwards, and sat down on the floor.

Then things went wild.

Desks banged.

Dried paint came out of the cupboard, and cascaded over everything.

Cacti were upset over desks, and the floor, and the gasping Miss Bodley.

The blackboard collapsed.

The windowblinds went up and down, and up and down.

The store-room tap began to run.

Something started throwing chalk.

Bang!

Crash!

"STOP IT!" yelled Miss Bodley.

A bucket came wobbling out of the store-room. It headed straight for Miss Bodley, levelled out and . . .

WOOOOOOSH!!!!

Somebody had dumped orange paint in the water. The mixture cascaded over Busy Bee Bodley, B.A., Headmistress of St. Thomas's School, Shore Street, Balmayne.

76

It covered her glasses and mingled with her red hair, turning it a sunshine shade. It soaked down into her cardigan and on to her tartan dress and her purple butterfly stockings.

"Oh . . . oh . . . " Miss Bodley sobbed.

Then . . .

"STOP IT! STOP IT! DO YOU HEAR!"

A child's voice was shouting. The desk-banging and blind-lifting and chalk-throwing and paint-dust-throwing and light-switching stopped.

"Go away!" the child commanded. "GO AWAY, you rotten thing!"

Bee Bodley took off her paint-blurred glasses and squinted at the child. It was Emma Small, the dentist's daughter.

"And don't you ever dare do anything like this again!" Emma said, looking as if she were going to burst into tears.

The classroom door closed softly, of its own accord. Emma came over to Miss Bodley, who was sitting on the floor getting her breath back.

"Are you all right, Miss?" Emma asked anxiously.

"Perfectly," Miss Bodley said, sounding anything but perfect. "I . . . er . . . there has been a . . . a . . . a little upset here, as you can see."

Miss Bodley got to her feet, rapidly pulling herself together, in the midst of her wrecked classroom.

"It's all right now, Miss," said Emma consolingly.

"All right?" said Miss Bodley. "Of course it is. Just a little . . . upset. An upset! Vandals or . . . or something."

"*Something,*" said Emma.

77

"You . . . you mustn't say anything to anyone about this . . . *upset* . . . Emma . . . people might not understand."

"Yes, Miss," said Emma, who knew all about people not understanding.

"Run along now, Emma," said Miss Bodley. "I will see to this myself." She sounded every minute more like the Headmistress Emma didn't like, and less like the frightened paint-bespattered woman Emma had rescued from the chaotic classroom minutes before.

"I could help, Miss," said Emma.

"No! No! You run along!" said Miss Bodley bravely. "I don't want you here if . . . I'd be better seeing to this myself."

Emma could see quite clearly what was going on in Miss Bodley's mind. She didn't want one of her pupils exposed to any danger. But in this case Emma knew all

about the danger. In one sense, it wasn't as bad as Miss Bodley supposed, and in another, it was much worse.

"Much worse, because *I'm* to blame!" Emma thought.

"Run along now, Emma!" Miss Bodley said. "That's an order!"

Emma looked round. It was *her* fault . . . the half of her that was the Other Emma had done it . . . there must be some way she could make up for it.

"Emma, GO!" said Miss Bodley.

"Just going, Miss," Emma said, but she didn't go. Instead, she picked up the board duster from the floor, went over to the blackboard, and rubbed everything out.

"Thank you, Emma," said Miss Bodley. "That was kind of you."

"I don't think it was very fair, writing those things, Miss," said Emma, meaning not just the writing, but everything else.

"Thank you," Miss Bodley repeated, in an odd voice. She turned away from Emma, and started to pick things up from the floor.

"You may go now, Emma," she said.

Emma picked up a piece of chalk from the floor, and turned to the board. She hesitated for a moment, and then she wrote:

I LIKE MISS BODLEY

right across the middle of the board, in large neat letters. Then she signed what she had written.

Signed:
EMMA KIRSTIE SMALL

"There!" she said. "Look, Miss."

Miss Bodley straightened up, and looked at the board. She stood looking at it for a long time, and then she said, "Kirstie is a very pretty name, Emma, I've always said so," in a funny voice, that seemed to come from somewhere in the back of her throat. "Thank you for the thought, dear!"

Emma went home, wondering what would happen next.

Chapter Twelve

The Emma Dilemma

"Emma!" Mrs. Small called. "Emma, come upstairs to your room at once!"

There was no mistaking the anger in her voice. Emma came upstairs, wondering what had happened this time.

"Your room, Emma!" said Mrs. Small grimly. "Look at it!"

Emma looked.

"It . . . it doesn't seem too bad to me," she said, with her heart in her boots. She wasn't wearing boots, but her heart would have been in them if she had been.

"Oh, doesn't it!" Mrs. Small said.

Then she took her daughter on a conducted tour.

Mud on the floor.

"My Busy Lizzie got spilled," Emma said.

"And seaweed? How did the seaweed get here?"

Emma had no answer for that one. Obviously her clean-up hadn't been very thorough.

"Your clothes, Emma!" said Mrs. Small, opening the top drawer in the chest of drawers. "And why, may

I ask, are the legs of your tights all knotted together?"

Emma had put her clothes back in their drawer hurriedly, and she hadn't managed to untie the tights.

"Have you been writing things on your mirror?" Mrs. Small demanded.

"I was trying to clean it," Emma said, looking unhappily at the smudged mirror.

"This is your room. *You* are responsible for keeping it clean and tidy. Nobody else!"

"I'll clean it up," Emma said.

"Quite right," said Mrs. Small. "You will! And you'll keep it that way."

Emma fetched the hoover upstairs, and set about cleaning her room, fuming inside.

"It isn't my fault! I didn't do all these things! It was HER!"

Half an hour later, when the room had passed inspection, Emma stormed out into the garden, looking for the Other Emma. She hopped over the wall into the Sherrys' garden and ran to the hut.

"Emma!" she shouted, dashing in.

Then she stopped.

The hut was sparkling clean. Someone had put flowers on the window-sill, in a milk bottle. The crates were neatly arranged, and the tyre armchairs had been straightened up. The floor had been brushed and the windows cleaned.

"Emma?" said Clare, coming into the hut.

"Oh, hullo!" said Emma, taken aback. "You haven't seen . . . " then she stopped, because she knew that Clare *hadn't* seen, because no one could see, except Emma and the Other Emma herself.

"Thank you for the flowers, and for making everything so nice, Emma," said Clare, smiling.

"Oh," said Emma.

"Now, I've got a surprise for you!" Clare said. She opened her cupboard, and took out a neatly ironed sheet. "Mum let me do it in the machine. I guessed you must have hidden it to get out of trouble, because it was all mussed up, and I made Mum promise not to say a word."

"Thank you," said Emma. "Thanks *very* much, Clare! I didn't know what I was going to do!"

"Now we can be friends again, Emma, can't we?" said Clare.

The Other Emma was flickering round Emma's room when she came up to bed, putting the final touches to the tidy up.

"Hullo," said Emma, coldly. "I'm glad you're doing something helpful for a change. It is about time, isn't it?"

The Other Emma flickered uncertainly.

"Promise you won't ever do anything like *those* things again!" said Emma, thinking of William, and Miss Bee Bodley, and the other people the Other Emma had frightened or upset.

"All right," said the Other Emma.

"Cross your heart and swear to die?"

The Other Emma crossed her heart with a transparent hand.

"I don't really want to play any more tricks," she said.

83

"Neither do I," said Emma. "It was my fault as much as yours."

They sat down on the bed, and looked at themselves in the mirror.

"Like two peas in a pod!" said the Other Emma.

"Uhuh!" Emma said.

"What are we going to do about *us?*" the flickering Emma said, with a shimmer of anxiety.

Neither of them had any answer.

"I'm fed up," the flickering Emma said. "Nobody can see me, and nobody talks to me. I'm lonely. Nobody likes me! Not even Dracula."

"I like you," said Emma, trying to keep up the Other Emma's spirits.

"You don't really count," said the Other Emma miserably.

"The Emma Dil-emma, that's us!" said Emma.

"I don't want to be a dilemma. I want to be me!" said the Other Emma, with another shimmer.

"You are you!" said Emma. "That's the problem. There's You-Me and Me-Me, and we're both the same person really, only there's two of us."

The two identical girls looked at each other.

"What are we going to do about us?" Emma asked.

Chapter Thirteen

Finders Keepers!

The family expedition to the Castle was scheduled for Sunday afternoon, as all their summer expeditions had to be.

Mr. Small had to work very hard six days a week in the Surgery. This meant that the Smalls couldn't get out together, except on a Sunday, so that is what they did.

They took a picnic to the Castle, which was about a mile away, on the cliffs above the town. Everybody took turns to carry the picnic, except the Other Emma.

"It would look funny, bits of a picnic going along on their own, Emma," Emma explained.

"I'm useless!" the Other Emma said, bitterly.

"You're not!" said Emma. "You're very good!"

"Am I?" said William, who had only caught the last sentence but thought it must be directed at him.

"Are you what?" asked Emma.

"Good," said William. "You said I was good. I didn't know I was being good."

"I didn't mean you," said Emma. "I meant . . . oh, nobody."

"Nobody" gave a sad shimmer, and didn't look at all pleased.

"I was talking to myself," Emma said.

"Emma was talking to herself, and she told herself she was very good!" William informed the others.

"In that case," said Mrs. Small, "Very Good Emma can go and get the ice cream."

Emma went to the ice cream van and bought five ice creams. They were cones, wrapped round with wax paper, and very awkward to hold.

As she walked back, one of the ice cream cones began to slip.

"Help!" Emma wailed.

William turned.

He saw the cone slip from Emma's grasp and begin to fall. Then it righted itself and flew back to Emma.

"Oh!" he said, blinking hard.

"I was juggling!" Emma said, quickly.

"I didn't know you could juggle," said William.

"Well, I can," said Emma. She handed William three of the ice creams to hold.

"Watch!" she said.

Emma held the two ice creams in front of her. One flew up out of her hand, and came down in her other hand, just as the second one left it.

William gasped.

"It's simple," Emma said.

It seemed that there was nothing Emma couldn't do with the ice creams. They spun and floated in the air and still, somehow, ended up back in her hands.

"There you are," said Emma. "Told you I could.

"Anyone can juggle," said William.

"Do it then!" said Emma.

William took the two ice creams. He looked at them, uncertainly.

"Do you . . . do you throw it?" he asked.

"Try," said Emma.

William pursed his lips, concentrated, waggled his hands and . . .

"What are you two doing?" said Mrs. Small. "You're keeping us all waiting."

"William has been juggling," said Emma.

"Well, don't!" said Mrs. Small. "That's quite enough of that."

A relieved William followed Emma and Mrs. Small up the hill after the others.

It was a long way to the Castle, up the cliff road, and their journey was interrupted by Jammy Ogle going past on his bicycle, and almost knocking William down.

"Careless!" Mr. Small said, with a frown.

"He meant it!" Mae said.

By the time they got to the Castle they were more than ready for the picnic.

"Now," said William, afterwards, "we storm the Castle!"

"You can't storm the Castle if there is no one to defend it!" said Emma.

"You defend it!" said William.

"Bet you can't sneak up without me spotting you!" said Emma cunningly.

"Bet I can!" said William.

But he couldn't. Emma seemed to have eyes everywhere.

"Zing! Aaaah! You're dead, William!" she exclaimed, for the fifth time, as her arrow pierced his chest whilst he was creeping round the moat. He had already been boiled in oil three times, and cut to pieces by her spears.

"How did you know I was over here, when you were watching over there?"

"I have ways of knowing these things," said Emma casually. "That's why I'm such an excellent Castle Defender!"

"I think you're cheating," said William, popping his thumb in his mouth.

"How?" said Emma.

"I don't know how," said William indistinctly, and for a moment he wondered about the juggling with the ice creams and the odd look on Emma's face when he caught her talking to herself. "I don't know," he said again.

"Never mind," said Emma. "I surrender the Castle."

"That means I win!" said William jumping up.

"You can be William the Conqueror," said Emma, and she went off to lie down on the grass.

Then it happened.

"My watch!" wailed William.

He came running out of the keep, and down the grassy slope towards Emma. "Emma! I think I've lost my watch!"

"Are you sure?" said Emma, propping herself up lazily on one elbow. She felt that she had done enough being-nice-to-William for one day. "Perhaps you didn't bring it with you?"

"Yes I did! I was using it to co-ordinate attacks!"

"You had no one to co-ordinate with!" said Emma.

"That doesn't matter," said William. "I know I had it with me. I *distinctly* remember having it. And now it's gone!"

"Tell Dad."

"I don't want to tell Dad," said William unhappily. "There'll be a row. I want to find it myself."

Emma got wearily to her feet.

"Come on," she said. "We'll take a quick look, and if we can't find it, then you'll have to tell Dad, whether you want to or not! Where do you think you had it last?"

"Up there," said William pointing. "Then I crept along the broken wall, and into the keep, and that was where you killed me."

"The fifth time," said Emma.

"It *must* have dropped off my wrist somewhere between there and the keep!"

They looked, but they couldn't find it.

"I don't want to tell Dad!" said William. "He said I'd only lose it! And I have!"

"Lost something, Fish Face?" a familiar, taunting voice cut across their conversation.

Emma whirled round.

Jammy Ogle was standing by the hole in the broken wall.

"I bet you lost something," Jammy said, and Emma caught a flash of gold as he waved something in his hand.

"That's my brother's watch!" Emma said, stepping towards him.

Jammy waved the watch in front of her nose.

"Is it?" he said. "That's not what I think, Fish Face! I think, *Finders Keepers!*"

"That's mine!" said William. "You give it back!"

"Finders Keepers!"

"Give it to me!" Emma demanded furiously.

"It's not yours now," said Jammy, picking up his bike from the ground. "It's mine. I found it. Finders Keepers! Everybody knows that!"

"That's stealing!" William said, almost crying. He grabbed hold of Jammy's handlebars. "You give me back my watch!"

"Let go of my bike, cry baby!" said Jammy, twisting the handlebars. But William wouldn't let go.

"I want that watch, Jammy," said Emma.

"You're not getting it!" said Jammy.

"Yes I am!" said Emma, and she grabbed for the watch.

Jammy went over under the weight of Emma's attack, and she and the bike and William went with him.

"Ouch! My leg!" Jammy shouted. He punched William, hard, and William was winded.

"I . . . want . . . that . . . watch! — " Emma said, pulling at the hand that held it.

Then

"Oau!"

"Ouch!"

"Aaay!"

Something strange was happening to Jammy. Someone was scratching him, and pulling his hair, and punching him, but he couldn't see who it was.

"Got it!" Emma said, as he let go of the watch.

"Gimme!" Jammy said, and made a grab for it.

He caught Emma, but he didn't catch the watch. It rose out of her hands, and bobbed in front of his nose, then . . .

"Aaaaah!" Jammy's head snapped back, as someone pulled his hair hard, from behind . . . *but there was no one behind him.*

"Ah! Ouuw! Oah! Ouch! Leggo!" Jammy struggled backwards, forgetting all about the watch in his efforts to get away.

"Give in?" Emma said.

"Ouch! Leggo. Yes . . . YEH!" Jammy yelled.

"You can stop now," Emma said.

The hair-pulling and kicking and scratching from nowhere stopped.

"Don't you touch me!" Jammy said, dragging his

bike from the ground. "Don't you dare touch me!"

"Run away, cowardy custard!" Emma said.

Jammy picked a stone off the broken wall, and threw it.

ZONK!

Emma took the full weight of the stone on her head. She staggered backwards and went down down into darkness, sinking . . .

Chapter Fourteen

Emma and Emma

"Emma!" the Other Emma's voice whispered urgently, as Emma sank into unconsciousness. *"Emma!"*

"Emma?" Emma murmured.

"We're all right again, Emma!" whispered the Other Emma, and this time her whisper faded as she spoke, and became an echo, echoing and echoing inside Emma.

"EMMA! EMMA!" It was Mr. Small's voice this time, coming from very far away.

Then she heard her mother say: "It's her head, Bertie. She's hurt her poor head again!"

And that was the last thing Emma remembered.

Chapter Fifteen

Emma Afterwards

"My watch was dancing, on its own!" said William.

Nobody took any notice.

They were all too busy fussing round Emma, who had been driven back home in Dr. Gibson's car, and was holding court on the sitting-room sofa, where she was the heroine of the hour.

"All on its own!" said William. "It danced! You ask Jammy!"

"Oh shut up, William," said Mae, who had no intention of asking Jammy Ogle anything, ever again, after what he had done to her sister.

"He's a bully," said Mr. Small. "And I've spoken to his father. Jammy won't be trying his tricks on my family again."

"Emma was talking to herself," William said. "Weren't you, Emma?"

"*William*," said Mae. "Nobody wants to hear your stupid little opinions."

"Don't be rude to William, Mae," said Mr. Small, automatically.

And so it went on. William couldn't get anyone to listen to him, and Jammy Ogle was too frightened by what had happened to complain.

Emma's secret was safe.

"I think it was very brave of you to stand up for William like that, Emma," Mr. Small said, and Emma glowed with pride.

"Heroine or not, it's time she got some sleep!" said Mrs. Small.

"But my headache's all gone now, Mum, really it has!"

"Aspirin, and bed!" said Mrs. Small.

Emma went upstairs, got into bed, and took her aspirin.

She was just swallowing it when Dracula put his head round the door and twitched his ears at her thoughtfully.

"Come on, Dracs!" she said.

Dracula sidled in.

"Come for your slippers?" Emma said, and she reached out of bed and put them exactly where Dracula liked them.

Dracula inspected the Snoopy slippers. Then he went for a prowl round the room, just to make sure It wasn't lurking somewhere.

"You're all right, Dracs!" said Emma, from the bed. "No more tricks! You're quite safe now!"

Dracula walked round the slippers.

"I won't so much as jump on you!" Emma said, and then she added, with a grin: "Unless I forget you're there, of course!"

There was something in the way she said it that made

Dracula hesitate. He considered the Emma on the bed carefully. There was nothing transparent about her.

"Goodnight, Dracs!" Emma said, and she switched off the light.

Dracula sat where he was, his green eyes glittering in the darkness, until long after Emma had gone to sleep. Then he got up from the slippers, stretched, and jumped up on to the bed, where he curled himself in a warm bundle just behind her back.

"Emma?" said Emma in her sleep.

But this time the only answer was a purr.